The Treehouse Gang

ALSO BY JON BUSH

Song of Laughing Moon 2016

Dragon Song and Other Poems 2017

101 Reasons to Love Betty 2018

Betty: Private Eye 2021

Pow Wow Sci Fi 2022

Rant 2022

Love Song 2022

Betty 2023

Persisting 2023

Rant II 2024

THE TREEHOUSE GANG

JON BUSH

FULL-SERVICE BOOK-MAKERS
ESTD 1999

PUBLISHED BY
The Chapel Hill Press, Inc., Chapel Hill, NC

ISBN 978-1-59715-294-5

First Printing
Printed in the United States of America

CONTENTS

My book, like a spirited horse, certainly holds some natural beauty, but needs to be corralled and tamed.

BACK STORY

My Mama

When I was little, I thought my mama was the most beautiful woman in the world. My early memories were of her immense kindness and charity. My brother Little Bear was too young to remember her well, but he still felt a deep sorrow the day she was gone.

She died in the Great Sickness of 1918. At least that was what Pappy told us. As a small child I had no reason to doubt that. But I was heartbroken. Pappy would hold me in his arms and say, "We'll get through this, Gracie. I'll protect you." It was not until I was in my early teens that I found out my mama had been placed in the white man's prison and died there from malnutrition. Now I was still very sad, but new feelings crept into my heart. They were of rage and anger. And every path led to the formation of the Tree House Gang—continuing her good work a few steps further, exacting what we knew in our hearts was justifiable revenge.

And no better companions could I have had than the Tree House Gang.

The Tree House Came

The Tree House came when Pappy wanted us to have some fun. So he bought some lumber, hammer and nails, a saw, and a ladder, and went to work. And after several weeks he had finished his project: a tree house.

It was in Indian school we met Lu Chang and Wilfred J. Lopez.

Lu Chang and Wilfred J. Lopez had grown up as orphans and now they lived in a boardinghouse. Rules were quite lax, and they could come and go as they pleased, all hours of the day and night, which suited them just fine.

Lu Chang remembered his mom from long ago, when he was just an infant, and how pretty she was. His dad had worked on the railroad. Both of his parents had died when he was very young, and he had been put in the orphanage. Life for him there had been difficult. The boardinghouse was a welcome reprieve.

Wilfred J. Lopez had lost his natural parents as well, and as a little boy he had been homeless. Then he came to the orphanage and bonded instantly with Lu Chang. There the two of them made a vow that, come whatever happened, they would have a better life. The boardinghouse was a step up, but not enough for these spirited teenagers. They wanted to live a full life, so they planted the seeds of what would become the Tree House Gang.

And when Little Bear and I came along, we saw Lu Chang and Wilfred J. Lopez had something special. And we had the Tree House.

The first meeting of us four was like magic. Each of us gushed with longings and dreams of glory. I, the only girl, became a natural leader. And I cajoled them to pace themselves, to sift through our goals, and to cultivate patience.

We established some guidelines. We all agreed we wanted to be a power of good. If our means were questionable, the ends were touched with the divine.

First thing, Little Bear and I made Lu Chang and Wilfred J. Lopez honorary Navajos. And it was agreed we would do whatever we could to help the People, the Navajos.

Lu Chang had this incredible ability to remain perfectly calm under the most stressful of situations. For this he was a natural front man for our schemes. If things began to deteriorate, for him it was just another day.

And his parents had worked on the railroad. His mother passed, and his father soon after. He firmly believed that rich white men had worked them to death.

For him the Tree House Gang was on a mission of true justice—and his fervor was infectious. Still, to look at him betrayed none of this. He appeared as calm as a warm, sunny day. But we who knew him were not fooled. He was the juggernaut for the Tree House Gang. His still water certainly ran deep.

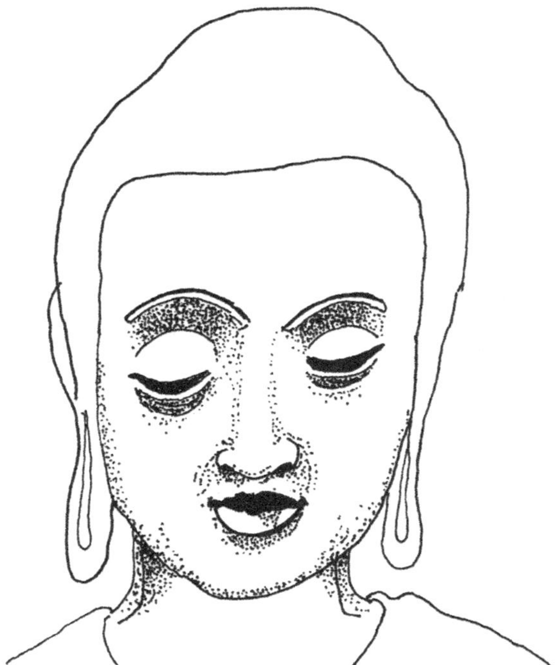

Wilfred J. Lopez

Silver-tongued orator,
With a natural ability to present falsehoods as facts—
He was so good at this that even I often did not know what
to believe from him.

Because of this we agreed on a special hand signal he would make if what he said was untrue. It was putting his forefinger touching his thumb with the other fingers clenched. If it was true he would put up the flat of his hand as if taking a vow. This proved to be very important.

Of course there were still many things none of us knew. For them, Wilfred would just hug himself. Nothing more needed to be said. For those things it was time to start investigating.

Little Bear was actually quite stocky. Although he might have seemed a little short on brain power, he was a whiz at picking locks and cracking safes. It was Pappy's brother Uncle Hojo who taught little Bear these things.

Uncle Hojo was a funny kind of guy in a good way. He was always careful to choose the right words for a troubling situation. If he disagreed with someone, he would simply say nothing. And if that person took that as an affirmation, that was fine with uncle Hojo. "One cannot have too many friends in life," he was fond of saying, "and after death, none of these things matter." Like Wilfred J. Lopez, he always seemed to have an uncanny gift to put just the right turn on the vernacular.

After he taught Little Bear, Little Bear was sworn to secrecy. "It's a gift to be only used for good." Hojo said. Respecting this boundary, I have only written broad outlines of these clandestine activities, safe cracking, and picking locks, and not the specifics. The latter is up to Little Bear to determine who has that ability and can be trusted to continue this art. If you will forgive my appallingly poor humor, with safe cracking, discretion is key

Little Bear's Stethoscope

Little Bear picked the lock to the local doctors' medical building and retrieved a stethoscope.

With this he would listen to the lock on a safe. He would turn the knob one direction until he heard the telltale click of a contact point. If he went completely around with no sound, he would turn it the other way until that tiny sound came. After this he turned it back and forth two more times extremely carefully. Most safes required three markers to be met and cleared to be opened, these going right-left-right, or left-right-left. And there was no margin for error.

How Little Bear knew all this has always left me mystified. The closest explanation I got from him was it was like approaching a rattlesnake. When that happened there was this great clarity of thought, all senses on alert. That was how he approached safe cracking. It was the most dangerous and subtle of activities. One wrong step and you were locked out—and the bankers would know the safe had been tampered with. Jail time would be in the offing.

It was up to me to forge signatures and handwriting. And it was a labor of love. I took great pride in my work. It was truly an artform that I approached with my own style. And I knew I was good, but I kept a level head and an even keel, because that was always for the best.

Our Clothes

I wore a colorful shawl my mama made for me made when I was very small, before she died. I never went anywhere without it. I also wore a traditional dress with a turquoise necklace and a belt of finely crafted silver ingots on leather that my uncle made me when I became a young woman. And I wore beaded moccasins.

Lu Chang wore a traditional Chinese robe, tied on with rope. This was over a shirt and pants. And he also wore slippers. Wilfred J. Lopez wore a Mexican shirt, stylish pants, and a beautifully woven poncho that depicted a farming scene.

By contrast, Little Bear only dressed in a T-shirt, work boots, and jeans. But he had a belt of abalone to honor his heritage. And when he worked at night, dressed in black, as we all did.

Our Headquarters

Our tree house was in back of my Pappy Teapot John's gas station on an ancient plain tree. It was hidden in the splay of the branches. It was entered by a rope ladder that could be raised and lowered as needed.

In the tree house were a wide assortment of tools and other paraphernalia, which included pen, paper, blank bank checks, bow and arrows, a skeleton key that would open many locks, and a jimmy that would open windows. Also we had food and drink and old comic books to read during downtime.

As I said, the Tree House Gang was committed to doing good deeds wherever they were needed. Every day after school we would meet and discuss the latest news, sifting the truth from rumors, talking about strategy for our current projects, and have a little fun. After all, we were kids.

Some things were relatively easy. The widow Elizabeth who lived alone often went hungry. We talked to Frank who owned a grocery store, and he gladly agreed to bring the widow food on a regular basis. She was so grateful. And that was all we needed from her.

Good Deeds by the Tree House Gang

Reading to blind people
Signing to deaf ones
Helping fellow students in many ways
Bringing mail to those who were housebound,
as well as food and company
Protecting kind and gentle souls
from cold and heartless bullies
All this and more with every day
We tackled with due modesty

A young boy named Lucas came to us saying he had been threatened by bullies after school. Little Bear walked with him that day. When the bullies came by, Little Bear said, "Anything happens to this boy, I'm on you like a fly to honey." And the bullies quickly drifted away. "Any trouble you have, Lucas," Little Bear said, "call me."

"Will you keep walking home with me?" Lucas asked timidly.

"Of course," Little Bear said.

And so it went. For the children who lived in an orphanage we found a clown to entertain them. As they burst into laughter our hearts were warmed. And where there was a need, there often was a solution.

Word got around about us, and it caught Sheriff Wylie's attention. One day he took

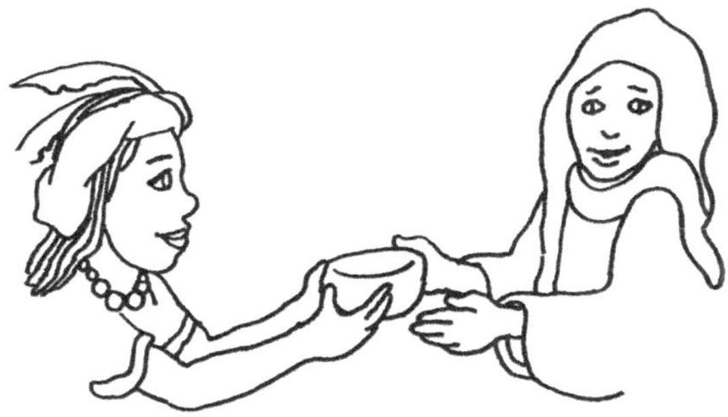

me aside. "I know you are good kids and mean well. But be careful. My job is to watch out for you." I was dutifully subdued, and he let me go with that warning. It was only some time later I would appreciate the danger we got into.

Lucas, Honorary Member, Tree House Gang

Lucas was so timid and shy. Our hearts went out to him. I convened a special meeting of The Gang, and we unanimously agreed to make Lucas an honorary member. The stipulation was that he would always have to have at least one other member of the Tree House Gang with him at all times for protection.

The Rules of the Game

Never steal from friends or family
Plan the smallest details
Always have an alibi
Never harm anyone
Keep a light touch
Lend a hand to those in need
Be happy when these tasks succeed

More Good Deeds by the Tree House Gang

For poor people I often forged bank checks, little enough so they wouldn't be noticed, and never more than a few at a time. It's called skimming, obviously against the law. But I was working for the power of good. And I never lost any sleep about it.

The Tree House Gang did little things, like

helping a blind man find his home
helping a young person with their homework
weeding and watering an elderly person's garden

On one of the more remarkable days, Little Bear was playing by the railroad tracks. Somehow he got his foot stuck between railroad ties. And just then a train was barreling down on him. I was too far away to do anything but scream.

Then, from out of the bushes, came The Stranger riding a pale horse. He wrestled Little Bear free. He took Little Bear safely to one side as the freight train roared by, whistles blowing and engineers scowling. Little Bear had a twisted ankle, but otherwise was healthy and hearty.

It turned out, though, that The Stranger was fleeing gambling debts of over a thousand dollars to a local casino.

We held an emergency meeting of the Tree House Gang.

What happened was that Little Bear and I brought a sack of worthless tin chips painted gold to the gambling establishment. Then we played some games. At the same time Lu

Chang went to fetch The Sheriff. Then the place was busted for serving minors.

And all debts were voided. The Stranger thanked us with a tear in his eye as he rode off, while we basked in the warm glow of a job well done.

Having "One Over" Them

A game we played was having "one over" someone. If a good friend forgot your birthday, you had one over them. If someone slept in instead of meeting with you, you had one over them. It was like getting a free pass the next time you were forgetful—or that you were superior by one. It was about a moment. If someone forgot to thank you for some kindness, you could take comfort in having one over them.

There were countless moments, mostly having to do with forgetfulness or crude behavior. Having one over them generally applied to small matters. Large and insidious wrongs were another story. Having one over someone was certainly about their guilt. And it was a way of taking comfort when forgotten or abused. You could say to yourself, *I had one over them*.

For us members of the Tree House Gang we all agreed we had one over the white people in their greediness and search for gold. We accepted what we had. As you might suspect, this game could become quite involved. For example, in picking locks, Little Bear could say he had one over the rest of us. And so on. Mostly this was all in good fun. And it led us to cultivate acceptance.

Pappy Was Never the Same

After Mama died, Pappy was never the same. Sometimes he would stare off into space. He took many naps. Often, late in the evening, I would hear him humming the mournful aria my mama used to sing to us at bedtime, and that was when the tears started for him.

When we were very young, Little Bear and I would snuggle up next to Pappy every night and comfort each other. As we grew older, we slept in our own rooms. But the feelings of Joss did not diminish.

We Said Prayers of the First People

Oh sister moon
Shine this starry night
Coming with us soon
To paint the land pale white

Oh brother dawn
Sing the sacred song
Shades of night are gone
Here where we belong

Oh father time
Help us with our need
To stop this wretched crime
And pull it like a weed

Oh mother earth
Let us sing anew
For what is true love worth?
If not for me and you

OUR FAVORITE TEACHER

How Anne Became Our Teacher

It wasn't until she was on the train west that the serious doubts began to sink in for her. Would she be accepted by her students? What were the living conditions? What were her intentions on this journey to the Navajo?

Anne looked out of the window at the countryside passing by, and the sun setting within beautiful pink and purple clouds. And as the train rolled onward to its destination, the rhythm of the wheels rocked steadily on the track. This motion lulled Anne into a fitful and uneasy sleep.

And she had three dreams:

The first one she was arrested and held with golden handcuffs
The second one she was riding across a plain with Buffalo

And the third one she was a little girl playing cowboys and Indians, and a Navajo woman came by and chided her, saying, "That's a white man's game." And Anne felt a deep flush of shame. And then the conductor came by saying, "Tickets." Anne realized she was almost at her destination and took her suitcase from the rack above the seat. As she struggled with it, she silently berated herself for bringing so much.

At that moment a handsome Native American man came by and said, "Can I help?" "Oh thank you, kind sir!" she gushed.

“I’m getting off the next stop.” He lifted her suitcase with ease and said. “It happens I’m getting off the next stop as well.”

“Do you know the area?” she asked.

“Born and raised there.”

“Can I trust you?”

“Who can we trust these days? Where are you headed?”

Anne gave him the address.

“Know it well,” he said. “I can guide you.”

Anne became very small and questioned with hesitation, “Shall I pay you?”

The man laughed and said, “Of course not.”

“Really?”

“You have much to learn about The People. And I can see you have come to help those in need.”

“Well, you don’t sound like a bad man, so I will simply say thank you so much. And you are a lifesaver.”

And with this kind stranger’s help, Anne H. arrived. He drifted into the obscurity of the Navajo nation.

Why Anne Chose the Navajo

When Anne was a young woman, her mother became deathly ill. The doctors said she only had months to live. Every so often Anne would burst into tears thinking about her mom.

One day she had a bout of crying on a trading post that was selling pottery and Navajo rugs. The shopkeeper, a young Navajo woman, asked Anne if she was okay. "It's my mom," Anne said. "She is dying."

"I see," said the shopkeeper. "I'm so sorry." She looked out at the desert. "Perhaps she could have a healing ceremony. I know of this medicine man. He is well respected. At the very least, he could guide her safely into the next world."

Anne tried to hide her doubt. "I mean no offense, but does that stuff really work?"

The shopkeeper bristled a tiny bit but then relented. "This shaman has healed many people. His name is Harry Okie."

"A white man's name."

"Oh, he's quite Navajo," said the shopkeeper.

Anne grew quiet, then said, "How do I find this man?"

And that is how so many years ago Harry did a healing ceremony for Anne's mom. And little by little she regained her strength and lived on for many good years.

Much later on her deathbed, Anne's mom's last words were, "Remember the Navajo." Anne would never forget this. Anne worked hard at school and became a journalist. Then one day she had an epiphany and saw her mom from the next world repeating the words "Remember the Navajo."

That was when Anne applied for a job teaching teenage Navajo children and was graciously accepted. These schools were designed to anglicize The People, the Navajo. Anne never had any intention of doing that. And that was when the trouble began.

The School Classes Taught by Anne H.

History—Navajo
Mathematics
Music/dance
Art weaving and sand painting
English

Anne taught students ages six through eighteen all in one big room. Obviously this was challenging—keeping the young ones interested and the older students from being bored. She did her level best at this, and with her compassion, everyone loved her.

Anne's husband had been killed in The Great War, the war to end all wars. They never had children, and Anne had never had an inclination to remarry. Her work was all that mattered to her, and her students were like her children. Anne would say that learning was the special joy of life. She always had time for her students, and she loved her work.

Anne was our favorite teacher. She was supposed to teach us the white man's way, but instead she taught us about our different cultures—Chinese, Latino, and the People's (the Navajo)—helping us appreciate our rich heritages.

Every day she brought us lunch and, with uncanny awareness, she knew what we liked.

Anne also taught English, though. "To survive in the white man's world you will need this," she would say. I was only lukewarm about English. I made many mistakes and found it hard to do the grammar. Anne certainly observed this and was rightfully concerned.

Anne took me aside one morning and said, "If you learn how to write properly in English, you can tell your story to many people. You are very bright."

Anne H. Teaches Me Writing

Mrs. H. had me writing a paragraph every day on whatever crossed my mind. It didn't need to be coherent or have any meaning. And this I would present to her, and she would accept it graciously. I knew she was being kind. I was just writing gibberish and gobbledygook. But I was writing. And that was the point.

With her encouragement I applied myself to learn English, as well as the culture of my people, Spanish, and Chinese. When I came across a word I did not understand, Anne would patiently explain it to me.

And every month Anne would bring in a different holy person from our tribe to discuss Navajo traditions and ceremonies. This was interspersed with Latino and Chinese mentors. "You have been denied your backgrounds," she would say. "I am here to awaken understanding, not shun it." For us these were the best of times.

But The Principal, Ernest Filmore, was a cruel man. He told Anne that she needed to cane her students. One auspicious day she took me into her office while The Principal was there. "I need to do my punishment in private," she said.

"Quite right," he said. "I'll just wait outside here."

We went inside, and I was trembling. Anne shut the door. She took a seat pillow and instructed me to cry out each time she hit it. And I did. What a relief! Anne truly was a special person. After a bit I walked out of the office as if in great pain; The Principal smiled at Anne. "Very good," was all he said.

He was not a stylish dresser. His pants always seemed a little short, his jacket tight, and his skin flaccid and pale. And he had no interest in our rich and vibrant cultures. He had been instructed by the higher-ups to "civilize the savages." And this was his credo. In all fairness, The Principal had begun his career meaning well. He had felt he was doing God's work, educating the Navajo in the white man's way to compete in the modern world of the 1920s. But life had been hard for him. The Principal was such a social misfit. And he actually knew little of what transpired in the classroom. He started each day with a few stiff shots of bootleg whiskey.

By noon he was tanked.

Things went along smoothly. Everyone was happy. Learning with Anne was infectious. The office pillow took many beatings. And we loved her so. Anne always made learning fun, with little games and humor. Like the word "lie" is in the word "believe." The word "war" is in the word "forward."

A favorite was the importance of the letter R. Without the letter R,

Friend became fiend
Bard became bad
Corn became con

Barn became ban
Pray became pay
Free became fee
Dried became died
Broom became boom
First became fist
Scrum became scum
and so on.

Anne taught us the enjoyment of language. How it can be serious, but also playful. And here I developed a love of poetry.

What happy times these were! But our beloved teacher was only to be in The Principal's good graces for a few short months. One rare day he peeked into class and heard us all laughing and smiling, singing a traditional Navajo ceremonial chant, and dancing in a circle. "What is this?" He ranted, "Where is history and math? Where are the classics?"

"They are just children," Anne said, "and they need to learn their background. Can't you have some compassion?"

"That's it," fumed The Principal. "Clear out your desk. You're fired!"

"You will be hated," Anne said.

"Good," he said, retiring to his office for a few stiff shots of hard liquor.

Getting Even for Anne

We held an emergency meeting of the Tree House Gang. "I have a plan," I said. "It's risky, but I think it will work." I outlined it. This was to be our boldest scheme. So far.

Before she left, I asked Anne if I could keep the letter of termination The Principal had written her. She was puzzled but agreed to it. "There will be retribution," I said.

"Be careful," she warned me.

Back at the Tree House I forged a note in The Principal's handwriting saying, with a riddle, "You'll never catch me, I'm a person of dignity." Just that. And no signature,

Our plan could only work at the darkest hour of night. Taking a large duffel bag we went to the bank. As I suspected, the night watchman was dozing. Working quickly and quietly, Little Bear picked the outside lock. Once inside, Little Bear picked the lock to the safe. We took out all the cash and left my forged note in the safe. Then Little Bear relocked everything.

But then as we were leaving, Lu Chang tripped over a milk bucket, making a clatter, and the night watchman stirred. Instinctively I tossed the bag full of cash behind some shrubbery.

“What are you kids doing here?” he growled.

“Just playing, sir,” Bill, the consummate actor, said.

“What’s in the bag?”

My heart froze. *He saw it, darn.* I turned to Lu Chang, and he was calm as always. We could have been talking about the weather.

“Just bats and balls,” Bill said, not missing a beat.

“Well, take your games somewhere else.”

“Yes, sir,” Bill said contritely.

We turned to leave, then the night watchman said, “Kind of late to be playing ball. It’s pitch black. Let’s see what’s in that bag.”

“Come look,” Bill said. I was shocked. I was having trouble breathing.

“I’m too old and fat to move,” said the watchman. “Show me.”

“Certainly,” said Bill. I was ready to die.

Bill gave the duffel bag a good shake and produced a bat and ball. *He’s a magician*, I thought to myself.

“Okay, okay,” said the night watchman. “Now get lost.”

It was only when we were safely away that I broached my big question to Bill. “How?”

“Always good to be prepared for contingencies.”

“What’s that?” said Little Bear.

“Trouble,” I said.

“It was a weak part of our plot, we needed a cover. So I added the bat and ball,” said Bill.

The next morning Frank the bank manager contacted The Sheriff. "Keep this to yourself." He said, "If word gets out about this, it could cause panic. Give things a few days. It's a small town, the truth will out. Let us lay a snare of silence. Remember, say nothing. Business as usual."

"Another thing," said Frank. "The robber left a note."

"Let me have it," said The Sheriff. "It's a lead."

"A third thing," said the manager. "The night watchman saw some kids lurking around."

"That's what kids do," said The Sheriff. "They don't rob banks."

"Maybe they saw something?"

"I'll make a note of that. Okay, keep your eyes and ears open and your mouth shut. No one's to know their hard-earned cash is gone."

"Of course."

"And Frank, take a bath or something. You look terrible."

"My bank has taken a bath."

"Stay focused, Frank. We'll get this. It just takes time. No reason to let your investors worry. Looking sharp is always a great asset. Let them know you're feeling flush."

"How about withdrawals?"

"Give me three days of silence, and after that we'll see what's what."

"They won't like this."

"Keep your eye on the big picture, Frank."

When The Principal woke up that morning, he was quite surprised to find so much money. And there was a note on top of it, saying, "From a well-wisher." Who could that be? He was mystified. But money was money. And money belonged in the bank.

Yes, The Principal was quite surprised to find so much money. On his meager salary he barely had enough for food and groceries. He decided he would accept this anonymous gift and deposit it in the bank.

When he arrived at the bank, he sensed a tension in the air. But he decided he was imagining that. He knew that he was thrilled with his cold hard cash—and anxious to begin spending it.

The teller was certainly startled. "A rich uncle left me this in his will," said The Principal. He signed a deposit slip, which for such a large sum the teller was required to show the manager.

The manager sat up straight when he saw the amount that was being deposited. It was identical to what had been stolen the night before. There could be no mistaking this. Frank contacted The Sheriff, who hurried over.

The Sheriff looked at the deposit slip. It

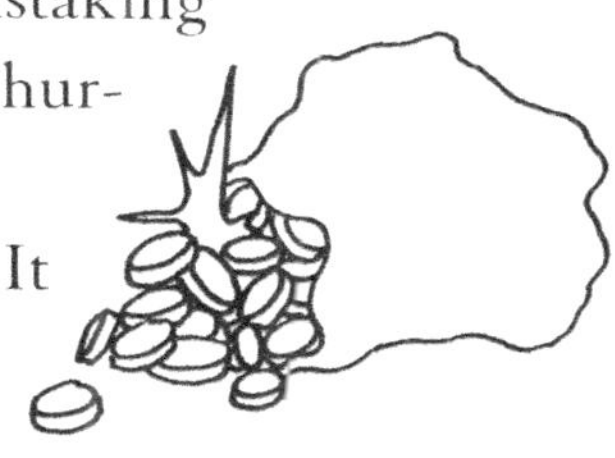

matched the writing on the note left in the safe. There could be no mistaking it.

We were at school when The Sheriff arrived with two deputies. They found their way to The Principal's office. And we listened in attentively outside the door.

"You are under arrest," announced The Sheriff to The Principal.

"I've been framed," he said. "I'm a good and God-fearing man."

"If you were indeed innocent, you would have reported the windfall to the authorities."

"But it was a gift."

The Sheriff continued unfazed.

"I have heard reports that you are generally mean spirited and cruel. Add to that, greedy and dishonest. And the note you left is irrefutable evidence."

The Principal was then out on bail. A trial was set. So far we had succeeded. Perhaps we felt a little sorry for The Principal, but not too sorry. Before his trial he skipped town with a cool five grand he had hidden away before going to the bank. In those days it was a small fortune.

We passed out a flyer that read as so:

TROUBLE SHOOTERS
AND PROBLEM FIXERS

Wilfred J. Lopez Lu Chang
Little Bear
Grace
Contact us at Indian School during
recess—between 10:00 and 10:30
Or slip a note during class
Discretion is guaranteed
Everything is under the table
Fees are minimal if at all

"What is 'discretion'?" asked Little Bear.

"Being careful," I said.

"We are that," he said.

Sky

And that was how we met Sky. A fierce warrior but a gentle friend, Sky was worshiped by every girl at school and feared by every boy.

I too was enraptured by his charisma and native charm. But I played it cool. So calm that one day he came up to me and said, "Why so cold, Grace?" I swallowed hard and was at a loss for words.

"Gee," I said, "I didn't think you would notice me, I mean. . . ."

"I heard you have some kind of club," he said.

"It's just a little thing," I said. "Wouldn't interest you."

"Try me," he said.

Now I really had to be careful. "Well, I would have to consult with the others."

"Of course," he said. And he gave me a wicked grin. *Don't swoon*, I told myself.

I realized I was staring at him with my jaw wide open. I quickly closed my mouth and said, "Our club is not for just anyone, and it's called the Tree House Gang."

"Right," he said. And he actually looked crestfallen. Silently I berated myself for being too harsh.

"Well," I said, "I could check with them, and see if you might visit." A little light shone in his eyes. And then it passed. *It must be rough being so strong and handsome*, I thought to myself.

"Don't strain yourself," he said and walked briskly away.

Gosh darn, I thought to myself, *I had the fish in my hand and I let it slip away*. In my mind I had been entertaining the idea of a relationship. Now that didn't look promising. Still, I decided to check in with the others and see if Sky would be copacetic, or at least acceptable as an observer, as Anne H. was. I now saw Sky as a challenge. There was a little glimmer of hope surrounding him. And even though in so many ways he was straight-arrow, we might have a use for him. His good looks spoke of innocence.

And that was always an asset in our work.

Accepting Sky?

When I first broached the idea of accepting Sky to the Tree House Gang, it was met with skepticism. Lu Chang and Wilfred J. Lopez had serious doubts about his integrity. "He's a glory boy," said Wilfred.

"And can he be trusted?" asked Lu.

"What special gift does he have to offer?" said Little Bear.

"I'm hearing all of this," I said. "His natural good looks are his asset. Women love him. He can open doors with his smile. As for the matter of trust, we'll do a special initiation ceremony. I have some ideas about this."

I expanded on my plan. Wilfred J. Lopez whistled softly. Little Bear and Lu Chang nodded their heads.

"I would say that's brilliant," responded Lu Chang, "and is what's needed."

"Sounds good," said Little Bear.

"Okay with me," answered Wilfred.

And with that we were on.

Sky's Initiation

The next day at school I went up to Sky and gave him a folded piece of paper. On it were written the four names of the Tree House Gang. "This is top secret, no one must know these. If this information leaks out, we will deny everything. Once you have read it, you must burn it."

Sky walked home with a little zip in his step. *Would I become a member?* he thought to himself. He did his homework, had dinner, destroyed the list with the names, and rested.

Later that night a shadowy figure in a dark cloak came up to Sky and said, "Tell me the names of the Tree House Gang and I will give you a big bag of gold."

"Who are you?" asked Sky.

"It doesn't matter, names for gold."

"I can't do that," said Sky. "I'm sworn to secrecy."

"Oh, come now. Everyone loves gold. Your people will never know."

"No can do. And how'd you get into my house?"

"Doesn't matter."

And then my joy burst out. I took off my mask and shrugged off the cloak. "Congratulations, Sky!" I said, "You have made the right choice. Now you are accepted."

Sky was confused.

"By refusing the money, you proved yourself to be worthy of the Tree House Gang. That was the test. You passed!"

"But how'd you find my house?"

"When you left school, the four of us followed you. Then

we went out for dinner and came back later. Little Bear picked the lock. Wilfred J. Lopez and Lu Chang kept watch. If you had accepted the money, we would have had a problem."

"Such as?"

"There never was any gold," I said.

"But I had your names," said Sky. "Didn't that mean anything?"

"Not likely."

"Why?"

"The names I gave you were not our real names."

"Do I get to know them now?"

"Of course."

Sky's Role in the Tree House Gang

Although Sky had passed the initiation in great style, he remained an observer like Anne H., showing up whenever a handsome face was required to sign some documents or greet guests to the Tree House Gang, or as a liaison to the banks and federal institutions.

Sky struck up a friendship with Lucas, and they shared many meals together after their various adventures in the white man's world of business and bureaucracy.

Suspicions

For a while things went smoothly. But it came to The Judge's attention that many Navajo were now able to buy groceries and new clothes, and even pay rent.

Yet at the same time, bank accounts weren't adding up. There had been a precipitous decline in spending capital. Every sign indicated robberies. The authorities decided that there would now be two guards at night instead of one. And newly designed combination locks would be put on the safe that were touted as pick-proof.

The newly moneyed Navajo were interrogated. Many didn't speak English, and the ones who did were deliberately obstinate. Lawmen found themselves increasingly frustrated. Searching for clues proved to be a tedious and fruitless activity.

After some heated debate between the local police departments, the feds were called in. Since the various heists had crossed state lines, they were now under federal jurisdiction.

The FBI—then as now—was nearly choking to death from the glut of mindless paperwork surrounding the most minor of illicit enterprises. Special Agent Bob was fresh from the academy, still possessing an untarnished optimism. His handler, Jasper, was a gnarled old veteran who had seen it all. When it was decided Bob would look into the Navajo, "Good luck, Bob," was all Jasper said, turning his head to spit.

Special Agent Bob headed to the reservation on horseback excited about his first case. But as he was riding, a rattlesnake reared up. Bob was thrown from his horse and broke his leg as the horse galloped off. Bob was in the middle of the desert all alone and hurting.

Fortuitously, Little Bear and I came up to him driving a Model-T from Pappy's gas station.

"Looks like you need help," commented Little Bear.

"Thank goodness you're here," ejaculated Bob.

"Right," I said. We took him to the reservation. Bob was moaning softly from intense pain. A shaman did a ceremony, and Bob was free from pain. Bob saw an elderly woman with a gold coin.

"Where did you get this?" he said. The old woman gave him a toothless grin and raised her arms to the sky, talking in Navajo.

"She is saying it came from Changing Woman, acting on behalf of The Great Spirit."

Bob examined the coin and said, "This is from a bank." He became lost in thought. Even in his desire for justice, he knew if he hadn't been picked up by the two young Navajo he could well have died.

It was then he entered himself as a biased and unreliable witness. And he left an open space in his report. How true it is that blank pages can say so much! And for the rest of his life he would be grateful to the First People. Bob's faith in human kindness never wavered.

The truth was that Bob had become emotionally involved with the plight of the Navajo. It wasn't said elsewhere, but Bob had become a friend to the tribe. His transformative experience in the desert introduced him to a spiritual outlook on life.

And this is how the FBI passed over some questionable actors in the theater of the Navajo nation. And The People welcomed Special Agent Bob at every turn.

THE "AUTHENTIC" CEREMONY

One of the Tree House Gang's most lucrative deceptions was that for a silver dollar, one could participate in an "authentic" Navajo ceremony. My Pappy had a piece of land he let us use next to the tree house. From Anne we had learned much of our heritage, and she provided us the traditional masks and costumes, pipes and drums, and our songs. For all appearances, it really was authentic.

It was a big success. Even the venerable tribal elders were impressed by our spirit. And they assisted us with the finer points. As always, it was by honorable subterfuge we enacted our retribution against the white man.

And tribal members could barely suppress a chuckle at what we were singing in Navajo:

Oh foolish white man
Giving us money for nothing
These words will never heal
Just spur us on to bring
All the white man down
This is the meaning of this sing.

The only people who knew these words were tribal members and good friends of the tribe. These included, of course, Anne. And she just smiled in her knowledge.

The Judge's Mansion

With brick and stone, Roman columns and grand archways, The Judge's mansion was an imposing sight, surrounded by lush gardens using the precious water that The Reservation so desperately needed.

His property was surrounded by an iron fence. Next to the front gate were statues of Greek and Roman gods. The gate was locked, and a guard sat in a hut next to that gate during the day.

If The Judge was fearful about being attacked, that was probably justified. In his tenure, many a poor soul had wound up at the end of a rope. And by far, most of them were Native Americans, including our beloved Uncle Hojo.

Uncle Hojo had been caught forging checks to get money to feed the poor people of The Tribe. He was sentenced to hang.

The Judge was a portly man, his cheeks pink from dining on prime rib and bootleg gin. He was used to getting his way. That was the unsaid expectation.

He was a cruel man. He handed out stiff penalties to hapless defendants who couldn't afford lawyers.

He was a firm believer in capital punishment. Over time he had accrued many enemies. They would cheer if he was foiled.

We found him despicable, loathing, and sickening. Little Bear and I vowed revenge for our beloved uncle.

A Climatic Moment

It was a dark and gloomy night indeed when Little Bear got caught picking the lock to the bank to do some skimming for the reservation's hungry children. For once, the bank guard was halfway sober and alert as he staggered over.

"You fooled me once," he said, "but not this time. I knew some cash was missing, just didn't know who took this. Now I know. It's you, ain't it?"

The rest of us were in the shadow nearby.

"Hush," I whispered to Bill and Lu Chang. "Won't do no good if we get caught too." And we had to quietly sit and wait as The Sheriff took Little Bear off to jail.

After the incident with Mrs. H. and The Principal, the Tree House Gang became the stuff of myth—mysterious and powerful. And The Judge's daughter Carolyn wanted to join us. Pudgy, spoiled rotten, Daddy's little princess, she was the worst kind of bully. She would steal her fellow students' lunch money and taunt them.

Smug and self-satisfied because her father was The Judge for Gallup, New Mexico, she was used to getting her way. But we stood firm, which drew her ire.

Then, after Little Bear was taken prisoner, that all changed. She was allowed to be a member. She gurgled with joy. But there was an initiation, we told her. To be a member, she needed to stay in the Tree House for twenty-four hours and not talk to anyone.

"But my parents will be worried," she said.

"We will talk to them and tell them you are doing an overnight. Remember, you must not see anyone until we decide you are qualified."

Carolyn began to pout.

"I don't know," she said.

"This a great honor," I said, "to belong to the Tree House Gang. And we will bring you candy."

"Really?" She brightened up a little bit. "I love candy."

"We know, all kids love candy. All you need is to sit tight for a day. And we won't harm you in any way."

Carolyn was drooling now, and there was this stench about her. With some effort I held back my disgust. I reminded myself we were doing all this for Little Bear. It was nothing personal.

We left a note at The Judge's mansion, saying, "If you release Little Bear, we will return your daughter Carolyn. Meet us by the bank at twelve noon with Little Bear, and you will have your daughter. Signed: The Tree House Gang."

When The Judge got word of the kidnapping he began to boil with rage. "If anything happens to Carolyn . . ."

"Give them Little Bear," said William Lawrence, the jailer. "It's not much, just another Indian for your daughter's safety."

"What has the world come to?" muttered The Judge.

"Negotiating with colored juvenile delinquents. I've heard of them—smug little devils." Then he said, "Okay, let's do it." The Judge had no idea where the tree house was where we had his daughter hidden. In fact, only a chosen few knew where our base of operations was. We worked carefully to keep it that way.

Stealthily we made our way with Carolyn to the bank at 11:40. Lu Chang and Bill Lopez scoured the surroundings for any hidden people. The coast was clear. That left Carolyn and me.

"Wait by the bank," I told her. "Your dad will pick you up at noon."

Before she could answer we blended into the greenery around the bank. We had hidden many times before.

The exchange was completed, and Little Bear slipped into the reservation, just another Indian.

"Did they hurt you?" asked The Judge.

"No, they were very nice to me. They gave me candy, and now I am a member of the Tree House Gang."

"No!" said The Judge forcefully. "And listen to me, young lady. This is not to be. Your mom and I have decided you will go back east to broaden your mind and curb your wandering spirit."

"No, Papa!" Carolyn cried.

But The Judge's word was final.

When she came to say goodbye, we couldn't help but feel

a little sad about her. She had been used. But she would live a life of privilege as The Judge's daughter. And she was mean and cruel. Mostly we felt relief that we wouldn't have to tell her she was not for us and never would be. We would not have to worry about Carolyn after that. She was on the next train to Boston.

But now we had to deal with The Judge.

A few days later, late at night from a hillside, Little Bear and I studied The Judge's mansion.

"Is there a way we could break in?" I asked Little Bear.

"Lamplight is always on," he said. "Hard to do."

We sat in silence. Lu Chang and Wilfred J. Lopez were on opposite corners, studying The Mansion from a hiding place, as we were.

Then at 2 a.m.: *Bingo!* A horse-drawn wagon pulled in and two people hopped off and knocked on the back door. It became very quiet. And then the door opened. We caught a glimpse of The Judge, and then the door slammed shut. The two people on the wagon began talking loudly to each other. Then the back door opened again and gunfire shattered the night. People jumped into the wagon and rode off cursing

"Wow," murmured Little Bear, "not a social call. Don't seem legal."

"Not for a judge," I said. "And it's pretty early in the morning."

The rest of the night was uneventful. The next day we rested.

Then we held a meeting of the Tree House Gang. I had been cogitating.

"I would say what we saw was not meant to be seen," I said.

"Then it's something illegal," said Lu Chang.

"And obviously it didn't go well," Wilfred responded."

"So what was it?" asked Little Bear.

"I have an idea," I said.

I was thinking of the stench surrounding Carolyn and I had placed it. It was alcohol. These were Prohibition years. Alcohol was illegal. How could The Judge's daughter have obtained booze? Was it connected with the drama of the other night? Pieces seemed to be falling together.

That night on a hunch we knocked on the back door of The Judge's mansion.

"Who's calling this late?" he said.

"We are here about some hooch," said Wilfred J. Lopez.

"I have no idea what you kids are talking about. Don't you know who I am? Get lost."

"We've talking to some of your buyers. They're saying you've been stiffing them."

"This entire conversation is ludicrous. You kids should be home in bed. And I am the judge of Tucson. I could have you put in jail, but I will let you go if you simply apologize for disrupting my rest."

"Okay," said Lu Chang, "but what about the gunfire the other night? Were you trying to kill our two people with the wagon or just scare them off? These are customers from high places. They are not looking kindly on this."

Before our eyes, The Judge began to melt. "I already talked to your people and it didn't go well. They were threatening me. I don't have the booze right now. I'm expecting the next shipment soon. You will get your order."

Wilfred J. Lopez smiled and said, "That's all we wanted to hear."

"Great," said The Judge, clearly relieved.

"Perhaps not so great for you," said Sheriff Wylie, emerging from the darkness. "Do I need to get a search warrant or will you come clean?"

Although it was cold out, The Judge was shocked and began to sweat copiously. He quickly searched for words. You could see the wheels turning. "Let's talk this through," he whimpered. "Surely we can make a deal? And keep this a matter between two gentlemanly persons of substance?"

The Sheriff, one of the good guys, brushed that off and said, "Cease your bootlegging and leave the Navajo people to decide their own affairs. Then you can still be The Judge for Tucson. That's the deal."

I didn't remember ever seeing a grown man fall so hard.

And the Tree House Gang now had The Judge in our pocket, which was fine all around, except, of course, for The Judge.

The Sheriff's wife Kathryn had passed away during the flu epidemic of 1918. He was devastated.

The Sheriff remarried some years later to a native woman

named Gentle Rain. They had two children who they raised in a combination of Native and Anglo traditions. He was considered a friend to the tribe.

And that was how, when we approached him with our suspicions, he said he would hear us out. We devised our trap under his watchful eye and, as shown, executed it to perfection.

THE TRAIN ROBBERY

We did many bank jobs
Our final job, a train robbery

The most ambitious heist of the Tree House Gang was a train robbery. It would take several years and many people to set up if it was done right. We were now well into our twenties. It was in the depth of the Great Depression. Never had the rich man been more despised. Many poor folk were cheering us on.

We agreed beforehand that this was to be our last accomplishment, our grand finale. It was as if we could sense law enforcement closing in around us. There were hints and suspicions, bloodhounds picking up an occasional scent, bank clerks who upon closer scrutiny were finding questionable deposits and withdrawals.

A single misstep on our part could prove to be disastrous. It had been a good run. Now it was time to close shop. There would be one last hurrah. And then it would be as if nothing had happened.

Joseph Wiggler was president of the Bank of Gallup, New Mexico. New Mexico had been admitted to statehood in the United States fifteen years before, but most of it was still wild—and part of it was the Navajo nation.

Wiggler was cut from the same cloth as The Judge, someone who enjoyed their sadism just for the sake of being mean. Any detriment to Wiggler would not be regretted by the vast majority of those he had taxed and squeezed into abject poverty.

He even had the audacity to charge rent from the Navajo on their own land. And there were so many Anglo and other people who despised his tyranny with money as well.

Little Bear applied for a job cleaning at the Bank of Gallup, New Mexico.

Little Bear came to the bank with a mop and a bucket and began to clean the dusty front steps. Then he took a rag and polished the bronze handrails. The president was summoned. "He's doing a great job!" The president asked, "Who hired him?"

Assistant Clemmons hemmed and hawed and seized the opening. "He just seemed right," he lied. No one had ever seen Little Bear before.

"Brilliant," said the president. "I've underestimated you, Clemmons. And we're paying him peanuts, right?"

"Naturally," said bootlicking Clemmons.

"Well, I'll leave you to it." And Wiggler headed into the bank.

Clemmons came over to Little Bear and said, "Looks like you got a job, boy. You speak English?"

Little Bear mumbled, "A little bit."

"Okay, be here tomorrow at eight for work."

"Thank you, sir," said Little Bear.

"Just make sure you show up," said Clemmons.

Little Bear was definitely going to show up. Once the assistant went into the bank, Little Bear quietly pumped his fist in victory. It was just one step toward the goal, but it was a big one.

Although these times at the bank were rife with suspicion and paranoia, Little Bear was considered harmless. People assumed he couldn't read, an appearance he carefully cultivated. He was given simple tasks that others abhorred or felt beneath them: cleaning toilets, mopping floors, taking out trash, and so forth. For his work he was paid but a pittance—and for his job he was considered an ideal employee, if he was thought of at all, which was rarely. His ingratiating demeanor served him well. And he seemed like the best kind of messenger: one who knew very little and therefore could be trusted with anything.

The numbers for the safe lock were changed on a daily basis. The president of the bank kept the combination for the day in a little drawer in his desk. Only two people knew the code: the transport supervisor for the train and him.

Every day at 8 a.m. sharp, Wiggler would give Little Bear an envelope to deliver to the transport supervisor with the code for the day and the scheduled shipping times for the gold. It was a power thing. This is how things were done at the bank. Simple things were made bureaucratic. A job for one was always extended into work for two or three.

The fact was that the president and the transport supervisor could barely tolerate each other. There was some deep-seated hatred between them, and many days would go by when they would never see each other. Little Bear would deliver any crucial correspondence between the two men that was required—and not one iota more. All they had in common was protecting the gold. They thought their system was foolproof.

In this way, Little Bear had his finger on the pulse of the bank. He would go to the janitor's closet and quickly copy these missives. Any information that he didn't understand he would run by me, and I would clarify it.

Looking when he wasn't seen, Little Bear discovered the mark he was seeking.

Five bags of gold were addressed to William McCutchen, H. D. Tucker, Edward Samuelson, George B. Withers, and Judge Oscar E. Farnsworth. These were shipped weekly by

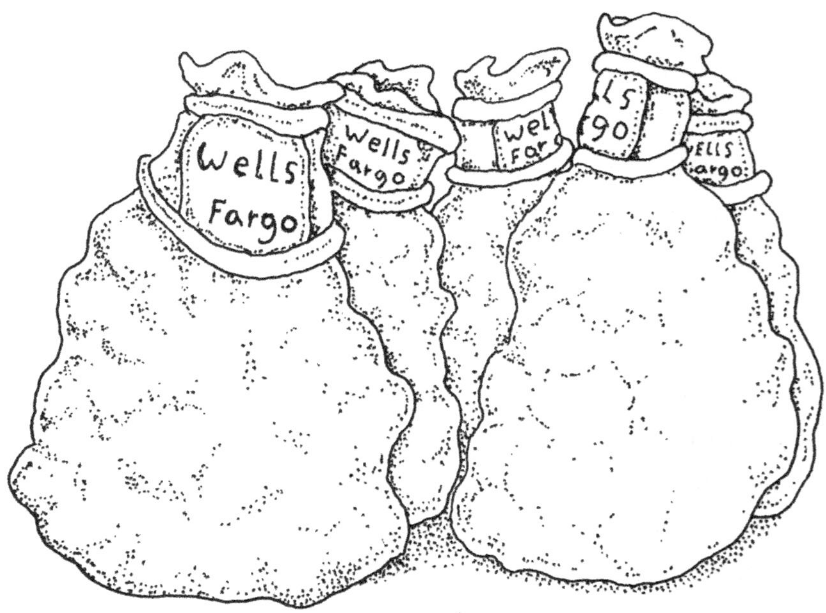

train from the Bank of Gallup, New Mexico.. In short time they arrived at Albuquerque. From there they were delivered to five different auxiliary banks surrounding the city.

After studying the bank's security guard for many nights, we learned he would take a break around 3 a.m. for half an hour, when it seemed there was no one around. And he always came back reeking of booze. After that, we could have set off a cannon and he would have been none the wiser. The president either didn't know or didn't care. It was difficult to get someone for the job of security at night. The bank didn't open until 7 a.m., which left a large window for our covert activity. It was assumed that no one could break in.

For the night of the robbery we chose New Year's Eve. All of the bank employees were getting drunk, including the president and the transport supervisor.

Little Bear had the key to the bank. We brought five wheelbarrows with grain bags filled with the rocks. Little Bear entered the daily code by spinning the knob on the lock. It opened.

We worked quickly but carefully. We transferred the gold into the grain bags and the rocks into the bank bags. Then we sealed the bank bags and left the bank bags filled with rocks in the vault. Little Bear carefully locked it using the same code in reverse, double checking to make sure everything was as we found it.

We carted out the grain bags filled with the gold in the wheelbarrows. We got outside and Little Bear locked the door. Then two drunken revelers came up to us, cute girls.

"What are you doing?" one asked. "It's late for bank business!" said the other menacingly. "What's in those bags?"

I froze. As always, Wilfred J. Lopez had something to say: "It's all about Happy New Year!" Then he and Lu Chang ran over to try and hug and kiss them. They recoiled in horror and disgust.

"Perverts!" said one. "Get off me!" yelled the other. And they ran off into the night.

I barely suppressed a laugh. But I knew we had to move things along quickly now because two pretty girls like those probably had boyfriends, and they wouldn't be happy.

A horse and buggy were waiting. We hoisted the gold onto the wagon and urged the horse on quickly.

Sure enough, the boyfriends emerged behind us. One yelled, "Want to take me on?" and the other yelled, "Leave our girls alone." But by now they were far behind us, and we were free.

We rode happily through the night to the reservation.

Working by moonlight, a group of trusted Navajos twisted apart the railroad tracks for the express train to Albuquerque delivering the gold at the projected place.

January 3, 1935

Tuesday, day of the delivery

In the morning, Wilfred, Lu, Little Bear, and me—all the members of the Tree House Gang—held a special meeting to make sure our schemes were all in place. Then each of us headed for our various posts.

2:35 p.m.

When the 2:40 express train to Albuquerque with the rock-filled bags was getting ready to leave, Wilfred J. Lopez snuck on board, as he had many times before with Lu Chang, while hatching the plan.

At 3:55 p.m., five minutes before the train was to be stopped, Wilfred J. Lopez rushed up to the guards and said breathlessly, "I think the engineer is having a heart attack. Come quick!" The two guards rousted themselves and made their way quickly to the front of the train.

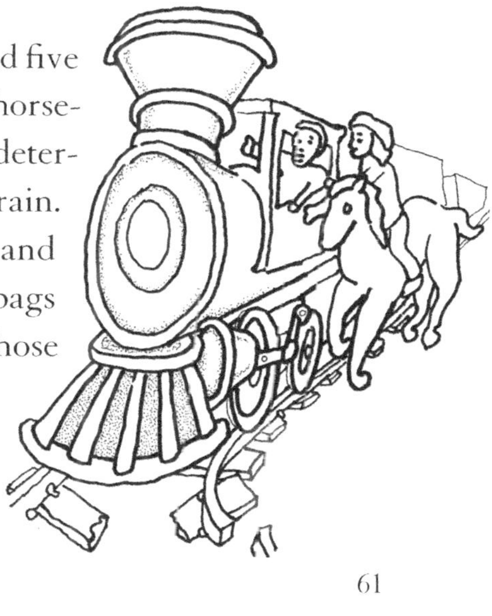

At 4 p.m. on the dot, Lu Chang and five enthusiastic Navajo warriors in six horse-drawn wagons arrived at the predetermined time and place, blocking the train.

Lu Chang checked the name and bank address of each of the five bags and set the Navajos in each of those directions.

When they arrived at their destinations, each bag had a note inside

of it, saying, "Courtesy of the real Americans, The First People, in payment for stealing the land of our ancestors." Robbing the train was simply to make some time for the trail of the real gold to grow cold, and as a special bonus to make a statement.

A Few Days Later

The Sheriff stopped by.

"You're smarter than four out of five officers of the law. But I'm not fooled. People have been coming up to me grateful for your help, in many cases with large sums of money I know you don't have."

"My job is to uphold the law. Perhaps you can explain what I am seeing."

"Sheriff," I said, "the Tree House Gang only provides for the poor and needy—those disenfranchised by rich white men."

"What does that mean?" Little Bear asked.

"It means to be deprived of basic rights," I explained.

"You can say that again." Little Bear said. "Right on sister."

"Okay," said The Sheriff. "These are troubled times. I'm willing to let some things slide. And you know I care for you kids, but be careful. I just don't want to see anyone get hurt. Don't make me have to make arrests. If I am forced to, I will."

I found myself looking at my shoes. "Yes, sir," I said.

"In the end you will have to answer to yourselves," The Sheriff said. "In my book, to feed the hungry is not much of a crime. That is money well spent. But between you and me, you don't want to get too well known. That's all I'm going to say."

And he walked away.

"Phew," said the normally reserved Lu Chang.

"Did he just say, 'Just don't get caught'?" asked Wilfred J. Lopez.

"What was that all about?" said Little Bear.

"I think his heart is with us and he is a good man. But he is conflicted."

"I'm confused," said Little Bear.

"As he said, he wants us to be careful, that's all," I said.

"That's all?" Wilfred J. Lopez said.

"And he will turn a blind eye, I think," I answered.

"And we can't pay him off," said Lu Chang.

"Not an option," I said.

"He is a good man," said Wilfred J. Lopez. "And sometimes good people suffer. Perhaps we could make him a gift."

"Excellent suggestion," said Lu Chang. "Perhaps a pie."

"I could bake a pie," I said.

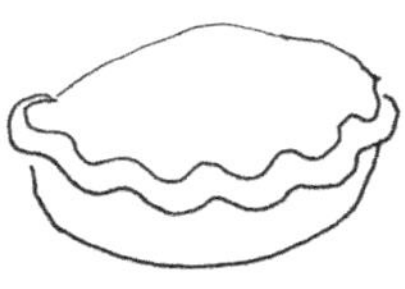

"I like pie," Little Bear chimed in.

"Of course you do," I said gently. "Maybe I could make one pie just for us, the other for The Sheriff."

"Great stuff," said Wilfred. "What do we always say?"

"Long live the Tree House Gang!" we all said.

Minor Details and Trivia

The Sheriff's family came over to America from Ireland during the great potato famine of the 1840s.

Seeking a land of plenty, they found themselves ostracized and rejected from places of work. As is well known, there were signs saying, "Irish need not apply." This bigotry left lasting scars. The Sheriff's father died a broken man. His last word to his son was, "Remember," and then he passed.

So, not unlike the members of the Tree House Gang, The Sheriff had his own reasons for despising the Anglos, known as WASPS. He had worked hard to become a law man, just and good. But he still kept a candle lit in his heart for the oppressed peoples of any race, creed, or background. This was because he would always "remember," which was clear, as his dying father had requested.

Grace, and the Return of Laughing Moon

When meeting someone there is a traditional moment of silence. Then the family clan is said.

My name is Grace.
My Pappy Pot John,
My Brother Little Bear,
My mama was Laughing Moon.

We all thought Mama was dead, until one glorious day she returned.

And she described her journey.

The first path I took was white with snow
The second path was green with flowers
The third path was the desert we know
The fourth path through the land that's ours
Each path offered these lessons to learn
That with an open heart I studied
And somehow I knew that I would return
Once again helping those in need

And I said,

Mama we are so glad you've returned
For me it's a dream come true
For your gentle touch how I have yearned
And the best of my life is in you

Lieutenant Josh Barrow and Laughing Moon II

What happened was . . . the US Army came and took my mama Laughing Moon II very far away. Later there was word she had died in prison. That also was not true.

In his vision, Lieutenant Josh Barrow saw a very bleak world without the Navajo. The skies and rivers were polluted with industrial waste. Children were crying. People walked downtown with vacant stares. All around was the sound of a funerary dirge.

Josh Barrow woke up in a cold sweat. *It was just a dream*, he thought to himself. And then he realized it was more than that. It had shaken his tree, and the sweet fruit of mercy was falling all around him, but still just out of reach.

Then he did something very strange for a white man in Indian country in the 1920s. He released all the prisoners he had been charged with. "Run for your lives, run!" he cried. Laughing Moon II was among these. As she passed by this kindhearted white man, she said, "I will offer a prayer for your wellbeing."

Lieutenant Josh Barrows was overcome with emotion and simply said, "Thanks."

Once all of the Indian prisoners had fled the stockade, Josh Barrow poured gasoline all around the building and lit it on fire. The story would be told how everyone here had burned alive, and Josh Barrows, suffering from great trauma, was honorably discharged. None of the Native Americans, including Laughing Moon II, were ever discovered.

Another Happy Ending

I was so glad to see my mama again. It was beyond words. I told her of all my adventures. She grew intensely quiet and then said, "We must take the high road with the white man and not stoop to his shenanigans and chicanery. Let me say I forgive you and applaud your spirit. But you must know this has to stop somewhere."

"Yes, Mama," I said somberly. "I have wondered this too."

"Perhaps you and your gang could practice charity work for the people, something legitimate."

"But that's not enough!" I blurted.

"I know," my mama said, "It's a thorny problem. I just don't want to think of my daughter as a criminal."

"This is a war," I said.

"Okay, I just don't want you to suffer as I did."

"You were my inspiration."

"I had my regrets."

"Please don't, Mama."

"I think I might have been a questionable role model."

"No, never. You were always beautiful—in everything you did."

There was a silence between us, and then Mama smiled at me and said, "You are truly my daughter, and I am so proud of you."

"That's all I ever wanted from you," I said.

"But please," she said, "be careful."

"Yes, Mama."

And we hugged like there was no tomorrow, and I shed a few tears of joy.

A Meeting of the Tribe about the Gold

The Elders convened a special meeting to talk about the large and mysterious influx of gold coming to the reservation. This must stop, it was decided. I actually felt relief at this. True to our integrity, our last robbery was of the train. Now we faced the tedium of everyday life. But we knew things could have turned out much worse. And we were free to go about as we pleased.

It had been a glorious adventure, the stuff of legend. Again and again we had put one over on the white man. And if nothing else, we had an outrageous story to tell.

Help for the People

Help for the People was the charity we formed for our people, the Navajo. As far as we knew, this title was unique. Days were spent soliciting contributions. We made phone calls, posted pamphlets, and knocked on doors.

Then we set up athletic competitions with entry fees. The winner would get a tidy sum. Next we organized blackjack and poker games. Before long we were very busy, this time legally. All the money we garnered went to the Navajo. And no longer did we have the stress of worrying that we would be caught, yet we still had the excitement of bringing in cash.

And the gratitude from the people we helped, as it had in the past, made it all worthwhile.

Book Learning

Ironically, as I write this, I believe the most important wisdom of life cannot be gained from book learning. Lasting knowledge is beyond the most illuminating of words strung together. What matters is the language of love and tenderness, gestures and symbols, alluding to unsaid emotions. In this sense, in how we communicate—even with the most passionate of poetry and the greatest of literature—there is always something a little extra that is undefinable.

Perhaps poetry is the closest connection to the reality of our sense of living as thinking and feeling people. Also, the great art of every culture speaks to everyone at some level. If we live a spiritual life, we accept that some things cannot be described logically—that our Higher Power "moves in mysterious ways." And that this is okay.

Still, I am not saying don't read. Please do! Books can be wonderful vehicles for stimulating and feeding ourselves and our imagination. Being able to read is such a great gift. Yes, I am a book writer.

Still, experiences in my life that have helped me grow and become what I am today have involved loving hugs, a fond look, a quiet moment shared, being accepted for who I am, going for a stroll through a beautiful garden . . . and countless other activities that promoted wellbeing.

But now in my hour of loneliness, having buried my life partner, writing my book has become like a dear friend with whom I am having a meaningful conversation. How I miss those hugs and kisses!

And the fact of our mortality looms larger than ever. It lends an urgency to my work. At my best, I am building a dream catcher with my prosaic writing, outlines of what we know to be true, containing that which leaves us with wonder.

ABOUT THE AUTHOR

Jon Bush worked for many years creating greeting cards and magazine covers. Only after the last ten years did he take on writing. He has published ten books and numerous chapbooks of poetry, as well as memoir pieces and individual poems. Two years ago he won first prize in a poetry contest. He was also included in *The Artists & Graphic Designers Market* in 2007.

Art and writing have given him great pleasure, and *The Tree House Gang* is one of his favorites.

Made in United States
North Haven, CT
19 June 2025

69964209R00049